DRAGON MASTERS

CURSE OF THE SHADOW DRAGON

WRITTEN BY

TRACEY WEST

ILLUSTRATED BY

GRAHAM HOWELLS

SCHOLASTIC INC.

DRAGON MASTERS

➤ Read All the Adventures ➤

1 2 3 4 5 6 7

8 9 10 11 12 13 14

15 16 17 18 19 20 21

22 23 24 *Special Edition!*

More books coming soon!

TABLE OF CONTENTS

FOR MY TALENTED FRIEND DIVYA SRINIVASAN

and her daughter, Uma, who would make an excellent Dragon Master.
Thanks for your encouragement and help! — TW

While Dragon Masters takes place in a fantasy world, many of the places and people resemble those here on Earth. The author would like to thank Vasudha Narayanan, Distinguished Professor of Religion and Director, Center for the Study of Hindu Traditions (CHiTra) at the University of Florida, for providing her expertise in the art and history of the Hindu people for this book.

Library of Congress Cataloging-in-Publication Data

Names: West, Tracey, 1965- author. | Howells, Graham, illustrator.
Title: Curse of the shadow dragon / by Tracey West ; illustrated by Graham Howells.
Description: First edition. | New York: Scholastic Inc., 2023. | Series: Dragon masters ; 23 |
Audience: Ages 6-8. | Audience: Grades 1-3. |
Summary: The Dragon Masters discover that a Shadow Dragon named Chaya and his Dragon Master Aruna are responsible for a huge shadow stretching across the sky, but how do they have so much power and why are other wizards around the world losing theirs?
Identifiers: LCCN 2022003482 (print) |
ISBN 9781338776942 (paperback) | ISBN 9781338776959 (hardcover) |
Subjects: CYAC: Dragons—Fiction. | Magic—Fiction. | Wizards—Fiction. |
Adventure and adventurers—Fiction. | Fantasy. | BISAC: JUVENILE FICTION / Readers / Chapter Books | JUVENILE FICTION / Action & Adventure /Pirates | LCGFT: Fantasy fiction.
Classification: LCC PZ7.W51937 Cw 2023 (print) |
DDC [Fic]—dc23
LC record available at https://lccn.loc.gov/2022003482

10 9 8 7 6 5 4 3 2 1   23 24 25 26 27

Printed in China   62
First edition, March 2023
Illustrated by Graham Howells
Edited by Katie Carella
Book design by Sarah Dvojack

THE STRANGE SHADOW

Drake and his Earth Dragon, Worm, stood in the Valley of Clouds. The wide, green space was tucked between King Roland's castle and some tall hills.

As Drake had hoped, Griffith the wizard was waiting for them there. So were his fellow Dragon Masters: Bo, Rori, and Ana. They had all planned to meet up for a picnic.

But the wizard and Dragon Masters did not greet Drake and Worm. They all stared up at the sky, frowning. A strange black shadow was creeping across the bright, blue sky.

"Is it nighttime already?" Drake asked, puzzled. "Those don't look like storm clouds."

Drake's Dragon Stone glowed as he heard Worm's voice inside his head.

It is not night. It is not a storm, Worm replied. *Something bad is coming . . .*

Drake gasped. "Griffith! Worm says that something bad is coming."

The wizard nodded. "I can feel it in my bones. Powerful magic is making this shadow."

"Ana, Bo, let's go get our dragons!" cried Rori, her green eyes shining. "We can fly up there for a closer look!"

Ana shuddered. "I don't want to get closer. There's something really weird about that shadow."

"Griffith, what should we do?" Bo asked.

The wizard stroked his long white beard. "Let me consult my gazing ball. I think—"

Everyone turned at the sound of galloping hooves. King Roland the Bold rode toward them on a chestnut-colored horse. The king was a big man with red hair, a bushy beard, and a tunic with a dragon symbol on it.

Dirt sprayed up as he brought the horse to a stop.

"Wizard, what is happening to the sky?" he asked in his booming voice. "My kingdom is in a panic!"

Before Griffith could answer, a bright light shone from above. Drake shielded his eyes.

A Silver Dragon flew down, ridden by a girl wearing a green Dragon Stone.

"Jean!" Drake called out.

The girl climbed down from her dragon, her metal armor clinking. A sword was tucked into her belt.

"Friends! I need your help!" Jean cried.

SOMETHING IS WRONG

What brings you here, Dragon Master?" King Roland asked Jean. "Who are you and where are you from?"

"I am Jean, a Dragon Master from the Land of Gallia," she replied with a bow. "And this is my dragon, Argent."

Drake stepped forward. "Your Majesty, Jean helped us save the world from the Naga."

King Roland raised an eyebrow. "That earthquake-making dragon? Then I indeed owe you a debt. And I will always aid Gallia, our neighboring land. What help do you need?"

"This shadow is covering our kingdom, too," Jean replied. "Our villagers are afraid. King Leon sent me here to ask if you will help us fight it."

King Roland frowned and gazed at the sky. "I fear I do not know how to battle a shadow."

Bo turned to Jean. "Did you get close to the shadow when you flew here?"

"We flew under it the whole way," Jean replied, "but Argent did not fly into it. He told me it was evil."

"Griffith, you said your gazing ball might tell us where that shadow came from," Rori reminded him.

Griffith nodded. "Yes, yes," he replied, snapping his fingers.

Normally his gazing ball would appear in his palm. Instead ... *poof!* A ball of blue yarn popped into his hand.

"This is no time for jokes, wizard!" King Roland snapped.

"This is not a joke, sire," Griffith replied. "Just a silly mistake."

The wizard narrowed his blue eyes in concentration and snapped his fingers again.

Poof! A large soap bubble floated above his palm. King Roland glared at him, and Griffith popped the bubble.

Then the wizard tried again.

Poof! A smooth wooden ball rested in his hand.

Drake frowned. *I've seen Griffith do a lot of magic, but he's never failed before,* he thought. *Something is very, very wrong!*

THE SHADOW DRAGON

The wizard frowned. "I'm not sure what is happening. Let us go to my workshop, where I can look for answers," Griffith said.

A royal guard galloped into the valley.

"Sire, angry villagers are surrounding the castle!" he announced.

"*Humph!*" King Roland huffed. "Any time something out of the ordinary happens, the villagers storm the castle. I'll deal with them."

He glared at Griffith. "And *you*, wizard, will solve this problem before things get out of hand."

Griffith bowed. "Yes, Your Majesty."

King Roland and the guard rode off.

Drake and the others walked toward the castle.

"It's nice to finally meet you," Ana told Jean. "I'm Ana."

"Nice to meet you, too," Jean replied. She turned to Drake. "Where is the silver sword I gave you?"

"Um, I don't usually carry it with me," Drake admitted. "I need that sword-fighting lesson you promised me."

They all traveled through the long tunnel that led to the Dragon Masters' Training Room.

"Wait here while we go into Griffith's Workshop," Drake told Worm, and Jean told Argent the same.

Inside the wizard's workshop, the shelves were filled with jars of liquids, herbs, and other spell ingredients.

Griffith walked to a large, clear glass ball and waved a hand over it. Magical light sparkled inside the ball, and a scene appeared.

A gray dragon stood on top of a temple with many towers. The dragon had two curved tusks and a long nose.

That dragon reminds me of an elephant I saw once, Drake thought.

The dragon's trunk-like nose pointed up, and a dark shadow streamed out of it and into the sky.

Next to the dragon stood a girl wearing a green, glowing Dragon Stone. She looked to be eight years old, but her long, braided hair was gray. Her eyes, as well as the dragon's eyes, shone with red light.

"A Shadow Dragon?!" Griffith cried. "But a Shadow Dragon shouldn't be able to create such a massive sky-shadow. This dragon's powers must be supercharged somehow."

"Look! The eyes of that dragon and Dragon Master are glowing red," Rori pointed out.

"Red is the color of evil magic!" Drake added. "Griffith, where is this Shadow Dragon? Do you recognize that temple?"

Before Griffith could answer, the light inside the gazing ball fizzled and popped. Then it went dark.

"It is what I feared," Griffith said. "My magic is not working, and this Shadow Dragon has something to do with it!"

CHAPTER 4

MIXED-UP MAGIC

"Could other wizards be having trouble with their magic, too?" Drake asked Griffith.

Griffith nodded. "I fear that this shadow may be affecting *all* wizard magic."

"Maybe Jayana, the Head Wizard, can help," Ana said. "She might know what's happening."

"Excellent idea, Ana!" Griffith said. "Drake, can you and Worm please transport to Belerion to speak with Jayana right away?"

Jean spoke up. "Argent and I will go, too. And you should bring your sword, Drake."

"Good idea!" Drake replied.

"Off with you two, then!" the wizard commanded. "Rori, Bo, and Ana, we shall go help King Roland calm the villagers."

Jean is strong and smart, Drake thought as he ran to his room. *I'm glad she's coming with us.*

Minutes later, he met Jean in the Training Room with a silver sword tucked into his belt.

Drake and Jean each put a hand on Worm. Jean put her other hand on Argent.

"Worm, please take us to the Castle of the Wizards in Belerion!" Drake cried.

Worm's body glowed, and Drake's stomach flip-flopped as they instantly transported to the castle. It sat on the edge of a cliff overlooking the sea. The weird shadow was creeping across the sky here, too.

They had landed outside the castle entrance. The doors were open, and unguarded.

"That's odd," Drake said. "Let's see what's going on! Dragons aren't usually allowed inside, but we might need them."

Drake and Jean entered the castle, followed by Worm and Argent. On a regular day, young wizards from all around the world would be in their classrooms, learning magic.

Instead, the hallways were filled with young wizards performing magic—or trying to. A few wizards were walking on the ceiling. Several of them had sprouted unicorn horns.

"Muzzlepop!" shouted a student next to Drake, and she waved her wand at a classmate stuck to the ceiling. The boy turned into a bird and flew away.

"Uh-oh," Drake said.

Then the Head Wizard marched down the hall, wearing an orange dress with fabric draped over her shoulder.

"Everyone must stop performing magic now!" Jayana commanded.

The students all stopped what they were doing.

Jayana approached Drake and Jean. "Drake, I assume you have come about this sky-shadow," she said. "Who is your friend?"

"I am Jean from the Land of Gallia, and this is my dragon, Argent," Jean said.

"And your dragons' powers are working?" Jayana asked.

Drake nodded. "Yes. Worm transported us here."

"Good!" Jayana said. "Then all is not lost."

"We came because Griffith saw a Shadow Dragon in his gazing ball. He thinks the sky-shadow is somehow connected to this dragon—and to the mixed-up magic," Drake explained.

"Hmm. So Griffith's magic isn't working, either," she replied. "Interesting!"

"Do you know what's happening?" Jean asked.

"I have seen this dragon in my gazing ball, too," Jayana explained. "I recognized the Temple of the Shadow Dragon in Sindhu, the land of my birth. You both must go there. With no wizard magic, dragons are the only ones who can stop the Shadow Dragon!"

CHAPTER 5

DARPAN

ean and I will head to Sindhu right away," Drake told the Head Wizard. "Can you message Griffith for us?"

"Yes. Our magic may not work, but our pigeons still do," Jayana replied. "I will tell Griffith where you are going."

"Great!" Drake said, and he and Jean got ready to transport. "Worm, take us to the Temple of the Shadow Dragon in Sindhu!"

They transported in a flash of green light.

21

Drake blinked. Here, the strange shadow completely covered the sky. In the near distance, Drake could make out the temple and the Shadow Dragon.

They had landed in a village. One- and two-story buildings lined the street they were on, but all the doors and shutters were closed.

"Where is everybody?" Drake wondered.

"Maybe they're afraid of the shadow?" Jean replied. Then she pointed down the road. "Look, there's a bright light in that building."

The Dragon Masters and their dragons made their way toward the small building at the end of the road. When they reached the door, which was partly open, Drake noticed stars and moons carved into the wood.

Is this a wizard's house? he guessed.

Jean knocked on the door. "Hello? Is someone here?"

"Come in!" a voice called from inside.

Drake turned to the dragons. "You two wait here."

The Dragon Masters stepped into the house. Right away, Drake knew his guess had been right. The place was filled with shelves of books, jars, and plants. A young, dark-haired boy stood by a desk.

The boy eyed the Dragon Masters' swords. "Are you soldiers? If you've come about the sky-shadow, it's no use," he said.

"I'm Jean, and this is Drake," Jean explained. "We're Dragon Masters. We've come from far away to try to stop the Shadow Dragon. What do you know about it?"

"Well, the dragon's name is Chaya, and his Dragon Master is my sister, Aruna. I'm Darpan," the boy replied. A sad look crossed his face. "But like I said, there is no way to stop Chaya. King Vikram's army tried and failed. I even tried to reason with Aruna, but she wouldn't listen."

"Is there a wizard we could speak with? Maybe the one who lives here?" Drake asked.

"Aruna's wizard disappeared around the same time Chaya began to create the sky-shadow," Darpan continued. "I came here, to his home, looking for answers. All I know is that something terrible has happened to my sister—and to Chaya!"

"Jean and I might be able to help more than you think," Drake said. "Come outside."

Darpan followed Drake and Jean. His eyes widened when he saw Worm and Argent.

"Dragons—of course!" Darpan said. "There may be hope after all."

A GENTLE DRAGON

ell us what happened to Aruna and Chaya," Jean said.

Darpan nodded. "The change in them both came suddenly," he began. "My sister is eight years old—only two years younger than I. She was always a smart, kind girl."

Drake thought of the red eyes of the girl in Griffith's gazing ball and shivered. Her eyes did not look kind at all.

"I was so happy when she became a Dragon Master," Darpan continued. "I knew she would be great at it. And she was. Aruna moved into the Temple of the Shadow Dragon to train with Chaya. They had a strong connection from the start."

"Did Chaya do something to change your sister?" Jean asked.

Darpan shook his head. "No, Chaya was sweet and gentle. He would cast shadows to cool down the villagers harvesting their crops in the hot sun. And he never left Aruna's side. She would always say, 'Chaya follows me around just like a shadow.'"

"That *is* very sweet," Drake remarked.

"Yes, but now they are both so different," Darpan said. "They have become very strange, and ... evil."

"We noticed their eyes are red," Drake said. "Could they have been cursed?"

Darpan nodded. "All I know for sure is that one day, the sky-shadow began to flow from Chaya's nose."

"It has reached our lands," Jean told him.

Darpan gazed at the sky. "The world cannot survive this sky-shadow. Plants will die. People will starve."

Drake looked at Jean and knew they were thinking the same thing.

"Jean and I will go to the temple," Drake said. "My dragon, Worm, can try to communicate with Chaya. If we find out what happened, maybe we can fix it."

"That is a good plan," Darpan replied. "I will keep looking for answers here."

Drake, Jean, and their dragons walked through the village to the temple steps.

Drake pointed to the top of the temple. "Worm, try to communicate with Chaya," he said.

Then he heard Worm's voice inside his head. *No time!*

The Shadow Dragon flew down from the roof, flapping his feathered wings. He had stopped making the sky-shadow, but it still hung overhead. Aruna rode on Chaya's back. The eyes of the girl and of the dragon blazed red.

"Stand back, attackers!" Aruna yelled.

ARUNA

haya the Shadow Dragon landed near the temple steps. Aruna jumped off his back and eyed Drake's and Jean's Dragon Stones.

"Leave now, Dragon Masters!" she said firmly. "Or we will be forced to battle you."

Jean's hand tightened on her sword. Sensing danger, Argent's scales flashed silver.

Drake stepped forward. "We are not here to battle," he said. "We just want to talk."

Aruna's red eyes flashed. "There is nothing to talk about!"

Drake quickly sent a thought to Worm's mind. *Worm, try to communicate with Chaya. Jean and I will work on Aruna.*

"Because you are Dragon Masters, I will give you a chance to escape," Aruna continued. "But I am losing patience."

"Aruna, we know something is wrong with you both," Jean blurted out.

"Ha!" Aruna scoffed. She glared at Jean. "There is nothing wrong with us! Everything is going right! Chaya's beautiful shadow will soon cover the world."

"Don't you see how dangerous that is?" Drake asked. "If the sky-shadow blocks out the sun, no crops will grow. People will starve. It'll be just like your brother, Darpan, told us."

"Darpan?" The red flickered in Aruna's eyes. For a split second, Drake saw the eyes behind the evil energy. Eyes that were brown and kind.

Is she fighting the evil inside her? Drake wondered.

"Yes, your brother, Darpan. He is very worried about you," Drake said.

Then he heard Worm's voice in his head.

I cannot communicate with Chaya. There is a cloud of evil magic blocking his thoughts.

Just then, Aruna's Dragon Stone glowed, and her red eyes flashed brightly once again.

"Your brown dragon is a spy!" she cried. "He tried to sneak into Chaya's mind!"

"No, Worm was only trying to communicate with Chaya!" Drake protested.

"Please listen!" Jean pleaded. "We can help you and Chaya!"

"Enough!" Aruna said. "I gave you a chance to flee, and you didn't take it."

Her Dragon Stone glowed as she gave her Shadow Dragon a command: "Chaya, release the shadow phantoms!"

THE SHADOW PHANTOMS

The Shadow Dragon reared back his head.

Drake tensed. *What is Chaya going to do?* he wondered.

A low humming noise came from the dragon as wispy shadows flowed from his mouth. The shadows quickly took shape into creatures with arms, yellow eyes, and creepy mouths.

Drake and Jean sprang into action.

"Worm, freeze those shadow phantoms!" Drake yelled.

"Argent, use your shine!" cried Jean.

The phantoms zoomed forward, extending their wispy arms. Drake felt a cold chill as they got closer.

Worm closed his eyes, and a green light spread across his body as he concentrated on freezing the phantoms. Then he shook his head.

I can't freeze them! he told Drake.

Suddenly, Argent let out a piercing shriek. He started to flap his wings.

A bright silver shine flowed from Argent's wings, pushing back the creatures.

Drake had seen Argent's shine power before. He could reflect any dragon's attack.

Now the shadow phantoms slammed back into Chaya. But the dragon simply gobbled them up! A burst of red light shot from his eyes.

"Fools!" Aruna cried with a wicked grin. "You have only made Chaya more powerful!"

Our dragons' powers aren't working against Chaya, Drake thought. *What can we do?*

There was no time for a backup plan. Chaya flew toward them. He flapped his wings, and a thick black shadow moved toward Drake, Jean, Worm, and Argent.

Goose bumps popped up on Drake's arms as he felt a cold chill again. The black shadow transformed into an eerie gray fog...

When the fog lifted, Drake, Jean, and their dragons were no longer on the temple steps. They were in some kind of desert, and everything around them looked gray. The sand and sky were gray, and there were no buildings, only strange gray plants.

Then Drake heard a voice behind them: "Welcome to the Shadow Realm."

THE WIZARD'S TALE

Drake, Jean, Worm, and Argent saw a man with a gray beard and gray eyes. In fact, his whole body was gray and sort of see-through.

Jean drew her sword and marched toward him.

"Who are you, and what is this place?" she asked.

The man shook his head, as if waking from a dream. "The Shadow Realm is a world created by Chaya the Shadow Dragon," he replied. "It is a prison from which no one can . . ." His voice trailed off, and he started to walk away.

Drake jogged after him. "Did Chaya send *you* here, too?" he asked.

The man blinked. "Oh yes, sorry. I am Vanad, Aruna's wizard. What has happened to Aruna and Chaya is my fault."

"Tell us what happened," Jean said, lowering her sword.

"I will show you," Vanad said. He held up a finger. "I have a little magic left."

He drew a circle in the air, and a faint light shimmered inside it. An image appeared—a golden flower with a red jewel in its center.

"I come from a long line of wizards," Vanad began. As he spoke, his body flickered briefly, like a candle flame. "One thousand years ago, one of my ancestors discovered the sprout of a Balam flower. Every thousand years, this special flower produces one seed."

In the image, the red jewel opened up to reveal a red seed.

"The seed gives great power to the one who eats it," Vanad continued. "Every time a wizard uses magic, the Balam seed absorbs their power. The seed will keep absorbing power until all wizards lose their magic."

Drake gasped. "So whoever eats the seed would have all the magic in the world, and nobody else would have any!"

Vanad stared at the flower. "I knew that the red jewel would open up during my lifetime. I counted down the days until I could be all-powerful. I told myself that I would do good things for the world. And while I waited for the seed, a Dragon Master came to train with me."

An image of Aruna appeared. Her hair was black, not gray, and her eyes were brown, as Drake had briefly seen.

"Aruna was a good student. We had happy times working together," Vanad said. "But soon I became distracted by the flower. I was eager for the seed to appear. I sat by the flower for hours, then days. I did not eat."

"Aruna must have been worried about you," Drake remarked.

Vanad nodded. "She was. And she knew something that I did not: No one should eat the Balam seed. Too much power is dangerous and tempting. Aruna believed that such a seed had to be a tool of evil magic. That the power would curse whoever ate the seed."

The golden flower appeared again, and its red center glowed brightly.

"Aruna tried to talk me out of eating the seed, but I would not listen. Becoming all-powerful was all I could think about," Vanad said. "And then, when the jewel opened, Aruna did something very brave—and very foolish."

A new scene played out inside the magic circle. The red jewel opened up, revealing the seed. Vanad reached for it. But Aruna's smaller hand grabbed it first. Vanad howled in anger as Aruna fed the seed to Chaya!

WE'RE DOOMED!

As the wizard's magic circle of light faded, Jean gasped. "Aruna fed the Balam seed to Chaya?!"

"Yes. Aruna believed that the seed's power would not work on dragons—only humans," Vanad said. "But the seed *did* work on Chaya— in a surprising way. The seed is supercharging Chaya's dragon powers. Chaya is absorbing wizard power from around the world."

"We've seen it happen," Jean said.

Vanad nodded. "And now Chaya can do things no other Shadow Dragon can do."

Drake looked around. "Like trap people in this Shadow Realm."

"And cast the whole world into shadow, and make shadow phantoms," Jean added.

"Yes," Vanad said. "And because Chaya and Aruna have a strong connection, Aruna has become filled with evil energy, too."

Drake shuddered. "That's scary."

"The evil of the seed has overtaken them," Vanad said. "My magic could not stop them. Then Chaya banished me here, to this Shadow Realm."

The wizard's body flickered again. He began to walk away, his feet floating over the sand.

Drake tapped him on the shoulder.

"We need more information," Drake said. "When we get out of here, how do we stop Chaya? Our dragons' powers don't work against him."

"We will never escape, but I will tell you what I know," Vanad replied. "First, if wizards all over the world stop trying to perform magic, they will stop feeding Chaya. He will still be strong, but he won't grow stronger."

It's a good thing Jayana told the wizards in Belerion to stop using magic, Drake thought.

"Then, there is just one dragon who can stop Chaya," Vanad continued. "A Star Dragon."

"I didn't know Star Dragons existed!" Drake remarked.

"They live high, high in the sky," Vanad said, and he got a dreamy look on his face as he gazed above.

"Focus, please, wizard," Jean said. "How can we find a Star Dragon?"

Vanad shook his head again. "A Star Dragon must come to you," he replied. "There is a scroll in my home that tells how to summon a Star Dragon. I was studying it when Chaya banished me."

"Then let's get out of here and study that scroll!" Jean said.

"Don't you think I've tried to leave here?" Vanad asked. "It can't be done. We're doomed!"

The wizard's body rippled.

"Er, Vanad, do you know that you're . . . flickering?" Drake asked.

"Of course I know!" the wizard snapped. "I have been in this world so long that I'm turning into a shadow!"

"Oh no!" Jean cried.

The wizard sat down on a rock. "It is my fate," he said with a sigh. "I accept it because of the terrible part I played in all this. But I am sorry that it is now your fate, too."

"It doesn't have to be," Drake said. "Quick! Everybody, touch Worm!"

Jean obeyed, but Vanad just stared at Drake, blank-eyed. Drake held the wizard's hand.

"Worm, transport us back to the Temple of the Shadow Dragon!" Drake cried.

Worm glowed green. Drake closed his eyes, waiting for his stomach to flip-flop.

Then Drake heard Worm's voice in his head.

I cannot transport out of the Shadow Realm!

THE ESCAPE

Worm says he can't transport us out of here," Drake told the others. "I think it's because this is a magical space."

"I told you," Vanad said, and he moved away from them, drifting.

"We are not giving up," Jean insisted. "There must be *some* way out of this Shadow Realm."

Drake and Jean looked around at the shadow desert. There was no sign of life in the distance. Above, the sky was covered in shadow.

"What if Argent tried to fly out of here?" Jean asked.

Vanad drifted toward them again. "You cannot fly back to the real world. Only magic can break you out of here. And what's left of my wizard magic is not strong enough."

Suddenly, Jean's eyes lit up. She turned to Drake. "It's time for a sword lesson!"

"What? Now?" Drake replied.

"Vanad's magic might not work, but your sword is magic, Drake," she reminded him. "You created a portal with it once, remember?"

Drake's eyes widened. He'd made a portal before to travel from the evil wizard Maldred's magical hideout to the Silver Lair. "The sword is connected to Argent's energy," he said.

"Right!" Jean agreed. "And Argent just used his powers outside the Temple of the Shadow Dragon. I think the sword can connect to that energy."

Drake held the silver sword in both hands. "It's worth a try," he said. He moved the sword in big circles in front of him. He made circle after circle.

Finally, the air swirled with silver light, and a portal appeared. Through it, Drake could see the steps of the temple.

"You did it, Drake!" Jean cried. "Let's go!"

Jean and Argent jumped through. Drake and Worm followed. But Vanad did not.

Drake looked back through the portal. "Vanad, hurry!" he urged the wizard.

"I can't go back," Vanad replied, and his body flickered once more. "I am a shadow now. Go! Find the Star Dragon! Save Aruna and Chaya—and the world..."

"Vanad, no!" Drake cried, but the wizard's body transformed into a wispy gray figure. Then the portal closed.

"He . . . he turned into a shadow," Drake said, still stunned. He remembered the time he had stuck himself with a magical shadow thorn. He had turned into a shadow, and it had felt very strange.

I can't imagine being a shadow forever, he thought.

Jean grabbed his arm. "Drake, we must get to Vanad's house and find that scroll!

Drake nodded, and he, Jean, Worm, and Argent headed to the wizard's home.

Behind them, twelve shadow phantoms followed, reaching toward them with ghostly arms...

FIND THE SCROLL!

Drake and Jean burst into Vanad's home, while their dragons waited outside. Darpan was still there, searching for clues to help his sister.

"Did you see Aruna? What happened?" the boy asked.

"It's a long story," Drake replied. "But we know a way to help Aruna and Chaya."

"Darpan, have you seen a scroll that mentions a Star Dragon?" Jean asked.

The boy rushed to a wooden chest in the corner of the room.

"Vanad's scrolls are in here!" Darpan said. He opened the lid.

Then Drake heard Worm inside his head.

We are under attack!

"Jean, come quickly!" Drake cried.

He ran to the front window, and Jean followed. Outside, a dozen shadow phantoms zoomed toward the dragons.

"What do we do?" Drake asked out loud. "Worm can't freeze them."

If Argent and I work together, I think we can stop them, Worm told him.

Drake told Jean what Worm had said, and she nodded.

"Argent, work with Worm!" she yelled. She turned back to Darpan. "Find the scroll! We'll protect you!"

"Will do!" Darpan called back.

Worm glowed green, and Argent glowed silver. A group of shadow phantoms charged toward them.

Then . . . a blinding, bright green light shone from Worm. Argent opened his wings.

Whoosh! Argent's shiny wings reflected the green light onto the attacking shadow phantoms. When the dazzling glow hit them, they dissolved!

"Worm and Argent did it!" Drake cheered.

Behind him, he heard Darpan call out, "I found the scroll!"

Drake turned to see Darpan holding a scroll. Behind Darpan, a shadow phantom floated through the wall!

"Watch out!" Drake yelled.

Darpan ran toward Drake, but the shadow phantom was fast. It reached toward the boy with its long, ghostly fingers.

Jean jumped between Darpan and the shadow phantom. "Back, foul fiend!" she yelled, and she pushed the phantom with her right hand. Suddenly, she gasped in pain.

Almost without thinking, Drake gripped his sword.

"Ahhhhhhhhhh!" With a mighty cry, he brought the sword down on the shadow phantom.

The creature vanished!

"Thank you, Drake," Jean said.

Darpan breathed out a sigh. "And thank *you*, Jean."

"Are you okay, Jean?" Drake asked. "Did that phantom hurt you?"

"It's nothing," she replied.

Then they all heard the beating of dragon wings. Drake, Jean, and Darpan ran outside. Worm and Argent were looking up at the sky.

Aruna and Chaya flew overhead.

"You may have escaped the Shadow Realm," Aruna said. "But you will not escape us!"

CHAPTER 13

HELP FROM AFAR

Chaya reared back his head, gearing up for an attack.

Drake, Jean, and Darpan ran and ducked down behind Worm and Argent.

Darpan thrust the scroll into Drake's hands. "Get out of here!"

"Come with us!" Drake urged.

Darpan shook his head. "I cannot leave my sister. Go. Find help. I'll be okay—Aruna won't hurt me."

Drake nodded.

Jean already had a hand on Worm and one on Argent. Drake touched his dragon.

"Worm! To the Training Room in Bracken!" he yelled.

Worm transported them back to King Roland's castle before Chaya could attack.

Griffith, Bo, Rori, and Ana greeted them.

"Did you find the Shadow Dragon?" Rori asked.

Drake and Jean told the story of Aruna and Chaya. They explained that the Shadow Dragon had been cursed with great power.

Drake held out the scroll. "We need to summon a Star Dragon," he said. "The instructions should be in this scroll."

"Let us study it in the classroom," Griffith suggested.

Before they could follow him, a circle of swirling, golden light appeared in the Training Room. A boy stepped through the portal. He wore a Dragon Stone, a white shirt, and an orange skirt. A gold parrot sat on his shoulder.

"Darma!" Drake cried.

The boy grinned as the portal closed behind him. "I sensed that you might need my help, friend," he said. "So Hema and I came."

The parrot flew off Darma's shoulder. Golden light exploded from it. When the light faded, a large, beautiful dragon stood in its place.

The Dragon Masters stared at Hema the Gold Dragon in wonder.

"Nice to meet you, Darma. I'm Bo," Bo said.

"And I'm Ana. Your dragon is beautiful," Ana added.

"We can use your help, Darma," Griffith said. "But tell me, how did you create that portal?"

"Hema and I have been practicing," Darma replied. "It is easy to find energy if you know where to look."

"Excellent!" Griffith said. "Now, let us study this scroll."

Drake held the scroll out to Jean. "You should unroll it," he said. "You saved Darpan from the shadow phantom."

"It will be an honor," Jean replied. She reached for the scroll.

Her hand passed right through the paper!

She gasped and held up her hand. It flickered, just like Vanad's body had.

"My hand ... it's a shadow!" she cried.

THE PHANTOM'S TOUCH

Jean's eyes widened as she stared at her hand. Griffith examined it.

"Your right hand does indeed appear to be a shadow," he said.

Jean's face clouded. "I touched the shadow phantom with this hand. When we made contact, I felt a weird shock."

"That's why you cried out!" Drake said.

Griffith frowned. "I think the touch of the shadow phantom has turned Jean's hand into a shadow."

Jean wiggled her fingers. "What if it won't stop at my hand? What if my whole body turns into a shadow, just like Vanad?"

"We won't let that happen!" Rori assured her.

Bo stepped forward. "Excuse me, but if the shadow phantoms were created by evil magic, then maybe Shu can help you, Jean. My Water Dragon has a very special power. Her mist can wash away any spell."

"Smart thinking, Bo!" Griffith said. "Fetch Shu immediately! Rori and Ana, please read the scroll in the meantime."

"Yes, Griffith!" the girls said.

Rori took the scroll, and the two girls ran into the classroom.

Jean was quiet and her face was pale as she and the others waited for Bo. Drake knew she was trying to be brave. He squeezed her left hand.

"It'll be okay," he promised.

"Yes," Darma said. "All will be as it should. I can feel it."

Jean took a deep breath. "I know I'll be fine with friends like you helping me."

Bo led Shu, a shimmering blue Water Dragon, into the Training Room.

"Hold out your hand, Jean," Bo instructed, and Jean obeyed.

Then Bo looked at his dragon. "Shu, use your healing mist!"

Shu closed her eyes. A misty blue cloud floated from her mouth. The mist rained onto Jean's shadow hand.

THE NEXT MOVE

Shu's healing mist sparkled on Jean's shadow hand.

"How does your hand feel?" Drake whispered.

"It ... it tingles," Jean replied.

The gray color began to leave her hand.

Jean flexed her fingers. "I think . . . I think it's working!" she said hopefully. Then her knees wobbled, and Drake steadied her.

"Oh no! Did I do something wrong?" Bo asked.

"You and Shu did well, Bo. The shadow phantom's touch has weakened Jean," Griffith explained. He touched her right hand, which now looked solid and firm. "She is cured, but she needs rest."

"Yes, rest, please," Jean agreed. "And thank you, Bo and Shu, for healing me!"

Rori and Ana ran out of the classroom.

"We learned something!" Rori announced. "In order to summon a Star Dragon from the sky, we need a Light Dragon."

"This book says we can find a Light Dragon on the Picland Islands," Ana finished.

Griffith paced as he thought of a plan. "First, we must stop feeding Chaya with power," he said. "Every wizard in the world must stop using magic! Rori, fly to Belerion with the news. Ana, go to Aragon to inform Diego. Then ask Carlos and the Lightning Dragon to help you spread the news."

Rori and Ana grinned.

"We're on it!" Rori cheered. Then she and Ana gave Griffith the book and the scroll, and raced to the Dragon Caves.

"Bo and Jean will stay with me to see what we can learn about Star Dragons," Griffith continued. "And Drake, at dawn you and Darma shall head out to find the Light Dragon."

Drake looked at Darma. "Your senses were right, Darma," he said. "We *do* need your help."

Darma closed his eyes. After a few seconds, he opened them. "I have something for you," Darma replied in his soft, calm voice.

Then he took an object from his pocket and gave it to Drake.

Drake studied it. It was a disc made of gold.

"Thank you," he said. "It is very pretty."

"It is also very useful, and you will need it," Darma said. "I sense that this will be a very challenging mission."

TRACEY WEST still can't believe that readers all around the world are discovering Dragon Masters. Her fans in India inspired the location for this book.

Tracey is the author of the *New York Times* bestselling Dragon Masters series; the Pixie Tricks series; and dozens more books for kids. She shares her home with her husband, her dogs, and a bunch of chickens. They live in the misty mountains of New York State, where it is easy to imagine dragons roaming free in the green hills.

GRAHAM HOWELLS lives with his wife and two sons in west Wales, a place full of castles, and legends of wizards and dragons.

There are many stories about the dragons of Wales. One story tells of a large, legless dragon—sort of like Worm! Graham's home is also near where Merlin the great wizard is said to lie asleep in a crystal cave.

Graham has illustrated several books. He has created artwork for film, television, and board games, too. Graham also writes stories for children. In 2009, he won the Tir Na N'Og award for *Merlin's Magical Creatures*.

DRAGON MASTERS
CURSE OF THE SHADOW DRAGON

Questions and Activities

The sky-shadow is dangerous because it is blocking the sun. Do some research! What would happen to Earth if we had no sun?

Wizards' magic is not working right because of the sky-shadow. Find three times that a spell goes wrong. Then write what *should've* happened and how the spells went wrong.

Aruna feeds the Balam seed to Chaya so that Vanad won't eat it. Do you think Aruna's choice is brave? Why or why not?

How does Drake's silver sword help him during this adventure? Reread pages 60-61.

Darpan stays behind when Jean and Drake transport back to King Roland's castle. Write and draw what you think happens next between Darpan and Aruna.